This book
belongs to

_____

BRADY BRADY

Superstar Hockey Collection

BRADY BRADY
Superstar Hockey Collection

Written by **Mary Shaw**
Illustrated by **Chuck Temple**

Scholastic Canada Ltd.
Toronto New York London Auckland Sydney
Mexico City New Delhi Hong Kong Buenos Aires

Scholastic Canada Ltd.
604 King Street West, Toronto, Ontario M5V 1E1, Canada

Scholastic Inc.
557 Broadway, New York, NY 10012, USA

Scholastic Australia Pty Limited
PO Box 579, Gosford, NSW 2250, Australia

Scholastic New Zealand Limited
Private Bag 94407, Botany, Manukau 2163, New Zealand

Scholastic Children's Books
Euston House, 24 Eversholt Street, London NW1 1DB, UK

www.scholastic.ca

Library and Archives Canada Cataloguing in Publication
Shaw, Mary, 1965-
[Novels. Selections]
Brady Brady superstar hockey collection / Mary Shaw ; illustrated by
Chuck Temple.
Contents: Brady Brady and the B team -- Brady Brady and the twirlin'
torpedo -- Brady Brady and the MVP -- Brady Brady and the super
skater -- Brady Brady and the big mistake.
ISBN 978-1-4431-4282-3 (bound)
I. Temple, Chuck, 1962-, illustrator II. Title.
PS8587.H3473A6 2015   jC813'.6   C2015-901175-2

Published by arrangement with Brady Brady Inc.

Brady Brady and The B Team. Text copyright © 2007 by Brady Brady Inc.
Illustrations copyright © 2007 by Brady Brady Inc.
Brady Brady and The Twirlin' Torpedo. Text copyright © 2002 by Brady Brady Inc.
Illustrations copyright © 2002 by Brady Brady Inc.
Brady Brady and The MVP. Text copyright © 2004 by Brady Brady Inc.
Illustrations copyright © 2004 by Brady Brady Inc.
Brady Brady and The Super Skater. Text copyright © 2005 by Brady Brady Inc.
Illustrations copyright © 2005 by Brady Brady Inc.
Brady Brady and The Big Mistake. Text copyright © 2002 by Brady Brady Inc.
Illustrations copyright © 2002 by Brady Brady Inc.

Collection copyright 2015 by Brady Brady Inc.

6 5 4 3 2 1   Printed in China 38   15 16 17 18 19

Contents

BRADY BRADY
and the MVP

Brady was always the first Icehog player at the rink.
He liked to get there early so he could high-five his teammates
as they walked into the dressing room.

The last and loudest Icehog to arrive was Kev.

At first, the Icehogs were concerned when Kev showed up after
everyone else all the time. They thought that maybe he didn't
take his hockey, or his team, seriously.

But each time Kev came bounding through the door with a
smile as big as the North Pole, they knew it was just his way of
letting everyone know he had arrived.

There wasn't anyone prouder of being an Icehog.

At practices, Kev drove the coach **crrraaazy!** — especially when he talked with his mouth guard in. With a wave, Kev would holler, "Eh Oach!" each time he skated by the bench.

Often, he would remind the coach that he didn't want to sweat too much during practice because "he was saving his energy for games."

This was when the coach would usually make him do an extra lap.

Brady found it amazing that Kev could talk as much as he did and still manage to put his equipment on correctly. Well, except for the time Kev forgot to take his skate guards off and fell in a heap as soon as he touched the ice.

Kev didn't miss a beat. He leaped to his feet and waved to the crowd to let them know that he was okay.

At the start of each game, Kev would skate over to the refs, introduce himself, and chat awhile. A few times, the ref had to skate Kev over to his bench so that they could get the game started on time!

When Kev finally took his spot on the bench,
the cheerleading began.

Always standing, Kev would yell to his teammates,
"Let's go Icehogs! Skate hard! Nice pass! Great job!"

He didn't just save the chit chat for his teammates.
His favourite thing to do was to race up the ice beside an opposing player and try to distract him.

Pointing up to the seats, Kev would say, "Hey, isn't that your granny in the stands?"

The player always looked up and always missed the pass.

Just as Kev was the last to show up before a game, he was also the last to leave. He liked to chat about the game with each of his teammates. So when everyone had already left the dressing room, there he sat, in full equipment.

At night as he lay in bed, Kev would think about hockey.

Like his friend Brady, he would dream about racing up the ice, sparks flying from his skates, and scoring the winning goal.

Kev never scored the winning goal.
Kev never scored any goals.
Nobody knew that this bothered Kev.
He kept this secret to himself.

One day after practice, the coach sat down next to Kev.

With a proud smile on his face, he said to his player, "Kev, the coach from another team wants to know if you'd like to play for them. They need another center for their top line. I'd hate to lose you, but you'd be getting a ton of ice time. It's your decision, but they need to know by tomorrow."

For the first time in his life, Kev was speechless.

He sat alone in the dressing room to think.

"Could I leave the Icehogs?" Kev said out loud.
But nobody was around to answer him.

Again that night, Kev dreamed about racing up the ice, sparks flying from his skates, and scoring the winning goal.

He was on the top line for his new team. He was one of the stars. This time when he woke up, he realized it didn't have to be a dream.

At the rink the next morning, the Icehogs waited for Kev to come bounding through the door — late as usual. They knew something was going on when it was the coach who walked through the door last, not Kev.

"Icehogs, we may have lost a player today. Kev has been asked to play for the Stars." As he headed toward the door, the coach said with a chuckle, "Make sure you don't pass him the puck!" The Icehogs were stunned. They knew the dressing room wouldn't be the same without Kev.

With his equipment slung over his shoulder, Kev walked slowly down the hallway toward the dressing rooms. He looked first at the Icehogs' door, and then at the Stars' door.

"I can't wait to score a huge goal!" said Kev . . .

and bounded through
the Icehogs' dressing room door!
"I'm **baaack!**" Kev announced, waving
his Icehogs jersey in the air.

Brady and the others cheered,

"We've got the power,
We've got the might,
Kev likes to chatter,
But he's always polite!"

Kev took his place beside the refs during warm up, making sure everything was set to go.

As he was escorted over to the bench, his cheering began.

"Let's go team! Play hard! Have fun!"

The Icehogs and the Stars battled hard, with the game ending in a tie.

Kev played his best game ever, but it was Brady who was awarded the MVP — the Most Valuable Player.

The teams lined up to shake hands. When Kev got to the end of the line, he turned to shake hands with his teammates. Brady reached out and grabbed Kev's hand.

"You were awesome!" he said to his smiling friend.

"Thanks, Brady Brady. I think I was too!" Kev laughed.

Brady's dad tucked him into bed that night. "Great game, son. Can I see your MVP puck?"

"Nope. I gave it to Kev. I thought he deserved it more — after all, doesn't MVP stand for Most Vocal Player?" Brady said with a wink, and rolled over to dream about hockey.

BRADY BRADY

and the Twirlin' Torpedo

Brady LOVED hockey. So did his friend Tes.
When they weren't with the other Icehogs,
they were usually on Brady's backyard rink,
practicing slapshots or stuffing pucks past Hatrick.

Brady thought it was great that a
girl LOVED hockey as much as he did.

At first, some of the Icehogs wondered about having a girl on the team.
That was before the Coach got Tes to show them her "Twirlin' Torpedo".

She . . .

*leapt into the air,
twirled in a full circle, landed,
and fired the puck with all her might!*

Chester never even saw it coming. Tes had always hated her
figure skating lessons, but those spins had finally come in handy.
She was welcomed to the team, and now she was an Icehog
like the rest of them.

Today, the Icehogs were playing an ***annoying*** team
called the Hounds.
Brady had been up since the crack of dawn.

He liked to be first at the rink so he could high-five
his teammates as they arrived.
As usual, Tes was the next one through the door.

When everyone was there and ready to play, the Icehogs huddled in the center of the dressing room for their team cheer.

"We've got the power,
We've got the might,
We've got the spirit . . .
Those Hounds won't bite!"

Both teams took their positions on the ice.
The referee dropped the puck and play began.
It was then that Brady and the others heard the teasing.

"What's a *girl* doing out here? Go home to your mommy,"
sneered one of the Hounds.

"Did you tie your skates in a pretty bow?" hollered another.
"Why don't you go home and play with your dolls?"

Brady looked at Tes. She just continued to play.
If she heard the heckling, she was doing a great job
of ignoring it.

43

"Don't listen," Brady said
when he sat on the bench beside Tes.
"You're as good a player as anyone here."

"Don't worry, Brady Brady. I'm not going to let them get to me!"
Tes replied. But when she went out for her next shift, the teasing
continued. And it got louder.

"Go home and bake some cookies," yelled a Hound.

"Make sure you don't break a nail!" barked his friend.

The taunts continued through the entire first period and into the second. Brady watched Tes. She was biting her bottom lip.

As hard as she tried,
Tes could not ignore the Hounds.
She couldn't concentrate. She missed passes.
She skated in the wrong direction.
She even tripped over the blueline!

When Tes tried her "Twirlin' Torpedo",
she fanned on the puck and fell down in a heap.
The Hounds laughed even harder.

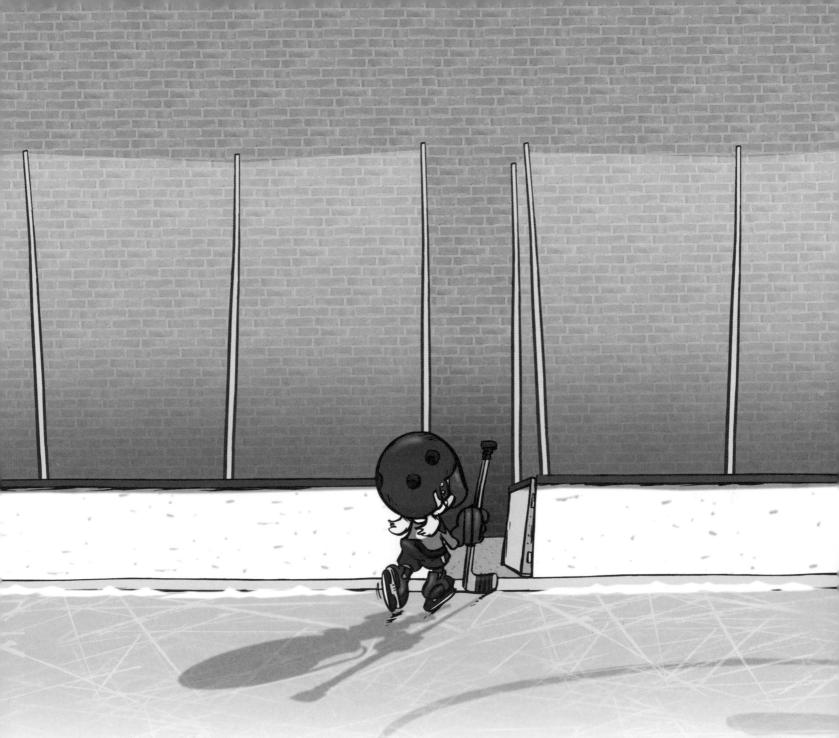

The buzzer sounded to end the second period,
and Tes was first off the ice.

In the dressing room, nobody knew what to say.
Tes looked sadly down at her skates.
"I guess I let you guys down," she whispered.

"No way! Nobody could play with all
that teasing going on!" Chester said.

"Right!" the other Icehogs chimed in.
"We'd be exactly the same, if it was us."

"Wait!" cried Brady. "That gives me a *great* idea!"

"All right, Brady Brady!"
The team huddled together to hear Brady's plan.

51

When the Icehogs skated out for the final period,
the Hounds just stood there with their mouths hanging open.
Some even rubbed their eyes to make sure they
weren't seeing things.

The Icehogs had a new look!
They had flipped their jerseys inside out,
tucked their hair up, and disguised their faces.

It was impossible to tell who was who!

"Let's play hockey!" Brady shouted, and the Icehogs flew into action.
They had never played so well — or laughed so much during a game!

The Hounds stopped teasing Tes because they couldn't tell which player she was!

Until . . .

. . . she lined up the puck
at the blueline,

leapt into the air,
twirled in a full circle,
landed,
and fired the puck with all her might!

Her "Twirlin' Torpedo" sailed right into the top corner of the Hounds' net, seconds before the buzzer sounded to end the game.

Tes had scored the winning goal!

The teams lined up to shake hands.
This time, the Hounds were first to skate off the ice with **their** heads hanging.

"Maybe they've gone looking for a girl to help them out," chuckled Brady, as he high-fived Tes.

Just then, the Hounds' goalie came back onto the ice.
He skated over to Tes. "Great game," he said.
"You mean, for a *girl*?" asked Tes.
"No. I mean *you* played a great game."
And a crowd of funny faces nodded in agreement.

BRADY BRADY
and the Big Mistake

It was the perfect afternoon for a game of
shinny — and the perfect place was Brady's backyard rink.

Brady shoveled off the ice rink and put out the nets.
He wanted everything to be just right for his friends.

That's when the idea hit him.

Brady flung his boots and mitts off at the back door, raced into the house and down the hall, straight to the room with the closed door. This was his dad's office. It was filled with stacks upon stacks of old hockey magazines, dusty trophies, hockey cards, and autographed pictures and programs.

But there was something that was more important than everything else.

It lay in a gold velvet case, smack in the middle of the desk. It was his father's special, signed puck. **This** puck had once been stick-handled and blasted into the net by his dad's idol . . . Number 4 . . . Bobby Orr!

Brady had been allowed to hold it lots of times, but only when his dad was there. This was different, but Brady told himself that his dad wouldn't mind. After all, pucks were meant to be played with.

Still, his hand trembled a little as he carefully lifted the puck out of its case. It felt warm in his cool fingers. He **had** to show it off to his friends!

Through the window, Brady could see them arriving.
Quickly, he stuffed the special puck in his pocket
and rushed to put his skates on.

"Hey everybody, check this out!" Brady hollered when he reached the yard. He held out the puck and the kids crowded around.

"What are we supposed to check out?"
Tes asked with a grin.
"It looks like a puck to me."

"Yeah," chuckled Tree. "We've seen a puck before, Brady Brady."

"Not this one, you haven't," said Brady, holding it higher. "This puck was used by Bobby Orr, one of the greatest hockey players ever! It's even signed by him," Brady boasted. "It's my dad's, and he won't mind if we try it out!"

As soon as he said it, Brady felt a butterfly in his stomach.
But then he saw the smiles on his teammates' faces.

He threw the puck onto the ice and tried to skate like Bobby
Orr. As fast as he could, he circled the rink, shifting the puck
from side to side on the end of his stick. Stopping in a spray of
snow, he was thrilled to see how impressed his friends were.

So, the game of shinny began. The Icehogs were **sure** the puck had special powers. Chester said it almost blew a hole right through his glovehand! Tes said her "Twirlin' Torpedo" slapshot sailed faster than ever!

And then . . . Brady got a breakaway.

Racing toward the net, he imagined that he was a famous hockey player carrying the puck up the ice for the big goal of the game. He took aim at the top corner of the net — and fired.

It went flying, over Chester, over the net,
and disappeared into the ***biggest*** snowbank in the whole backyard!

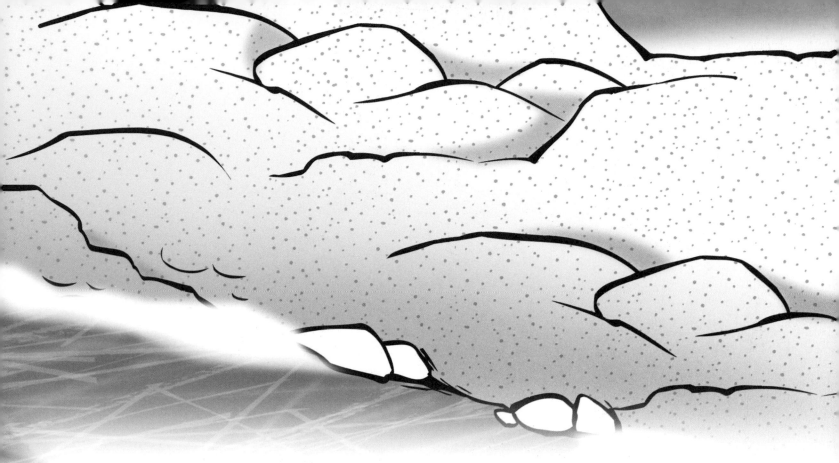

Everything stopped. Everyone fell silent.

Beads of sweat trickled down Brady's face, but they weren't from his breakaway. They were from the thought of his dad's special Bobby Orr puck *lost* in all that snow.

Brady and his teammates scrambled over the smaller snowbanks and into the *huge* pile of snow that had swallowed the puck.

"We'd better hurry up and find it," Brady said. "The street lights are coming on. That means my dad will be home soon."

Snow flew every which way as the Icehogs frantically searched for the missing puck.

One by one, they flopped, exhausted, into the snow.

"**What** am I going to tell my dad?" Brady cried, burying his face in his hands.

"Maybe you could tell him Bobby Orr called and asked for his puck back," Tree suggested, trying to be helpful.

"You could tell him that you took it to a sports store to get the nicks and scrapes repaired," offered Chester.

Brady looked up at the pile of snow.
How could he have made such a big mistake?

His father had taken special care of that puck because it meant so much to him. Brady hadn't thought about how his dad might feel knowing his prized puck was being whacked around on the ice. He had only thought about how *he* would feel showing it off to his friends.

Brady heard the car pull into the driveway. He couldn't move. His friends felt badly for him, wondering what he was going to tell his dad.

Brady's dad walked into the backyard.

"Hi kids! Having fun?" he asked. But nobody answered. They couldn't even look at him.

Then in the silence, a small voice spoke up.

"I need to tell you something, Dad," Brady mumbled, "and you're not going to like it." Brady's eyes met his father's. "You know your autographed puck that I'm just supposed to *look* at? Well, I did more than *look* at it. I picked it up."

Brady's dad grinned knowingly and nodded. "I understand, Brady Brady. It's hard not to want to pick it up. It's pretty special."

Brady interrupted. "I didn't just pick it up, though, Dad. I told the kids that we could play with it . . . I took a wrist shot . . ." Brady gulped. ". . . a wrist shot right into that *huge* snowbank!"

Brady and his friends all pointed at the sinister heap.

His dad's smile disappeared, and his eyes blinked in disbelief. At that moment, Brady was afraid he had broken his father's trust **and** his heart.

"I'm really, really sorry. Even if it takes me until spring, I won't stop looking for that puck," Brady said.

Brady's dad squeezed his shoulder and looked at him.

"To be honest, I am disappointed that you took the puck without my permission. But believe it or not, Brady Brady, your telling me the truth about what happened means more to me than any puck — even that one. And do you know what else?" he added. "You won't have to look for it until spring. I'll help you now." Brady's dad gave him a wink.

"Why don't we start by looking in Hatrick's doghouse!"

BRADY BRADY
and the Super Skater

Brady couldn't wait to get to the rink. His coach had promised two things for today's practice — a scrimmage game and a new teammate for the Icehogs.

As Brady walked through the parking lot, he noticed a yellow car.
Inside there was a flurry of activity; equipment was flying
everywhere! Helmet, gloves, pants, pads, pucks, and leotards!

"Leotards?!" Brady said with surprise.

Suddenly the car door swung open. "Hurry up, Caroline, you'll be late for your hockey practice," said a woman, as she accidentally dropped a ballet slipper in the slush.

"I know, I know — and my hair is such a mess!" replied a voice from the back seat.

Brady watched as a girl with a headful of curls jumped out of the car, hockey stick in hand.

He rushed ahead to open the door for her. "Hi, I'm Brady," he said proudly. "My friends call me Brady Brady."

"Thank you Brady Brady," she said, flashing a smile. Brady could feel his cheeks turning red. "I'm Caroline and I'm going to be playing for the Icehogs."

When they arrived at the dressing room, the coach asked Brady
to introduce Caroline to the rest of the team.

Brady high-fived his teammates as they arrived, and introduced Caroline as their newest player. Caroline looked around at her teammates and took a seat beside Chester.

As the team got dressed for practice, Caroline brushed her hair anxiously. "I know a helmet is a great thing to wear to keep my brain safe, but it makes a terrible mess of my curls!" she said with a giggle.

"Don't be nervous, Caroline," Brady told her. "You'll do fine."
But Caroline didn't feel fine.

On the ice, Caroline took off like a rocket!
The Icehogs could not believe how fast she could skate!

"Hey!" Brady called as he tried to catch up to her.
"Where did you learn to be such a super skater?"
But Caroline didn't answer; she was focused on her skating.

Brady's favorite part of practice was the team scrimmage.
The Icehogs were split into two groups.

Brady raced up the ice with Caroline heading toward the net.
He fed her a perfect pass — but it went right past her stick. When she
finally did get the puck, she fired it at Chester — but it went *waaay*
off to the side of the net. "That's okay," Brady reassured her.
"We'll get it next time."

But the next time,
Caroline missed the net again.

And again.

And again.

Brady had never seen
such horrible luck.

Even Chester felt bad for her
and hoped she would get one past him.

In the dressing room, Caroline didn't seem to mind that she had missed the net so often. She proudly showed her new teammates the biggest ball of hockey tape anyone had ever seen!

When the others took the tape off of their socks, they handed it to Caroline. She smiled as she added it to her tape ball. Caroline knew she was going to love being a member of the Icehogs.

"See everyone at the game tomorrow," she waved as she headed out the door. But when she got into her mother's car, Caroline twirled her hair nervously. She wasn't so sure she was looking forward to tomorrow...

On game day, Brady and Caroline waved at Chester who was
munching on popcorn in the concession stand.

"Come on, Chester, game time," Brady called to his friend
with a chuckle.

Caroline took a seat in the corner of the dressing room.
Slowly, she took out her skates.

"Hey, Caroline, why don't we toss your tape ball around while we
wait for the others?" Brady suggested, hoping
to make her less nervous.

As Brady helped Caroline pull the huge ball out of the bag, he noticed a clear case with a pair of eyeglasses in it.

"Hey, I didn't know you wore glasses!" Brady said to Caroline.

"Uh...I don't!" she said, snatching the case out of his hand. "They're for...uh...dressing up my tape ball."

Plopping the tape ball on the bench, she placed the glasses on it. "See? Just like a snowman!"

Chester pointed at the tape ball and burst out laughing.
"Hey, it kinda looks like me!" he said.

Caroline quickly put her glasses back in the case and buried them deep in her bag.

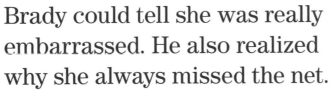

Brady could tell she was really embarrassed. He also realized why she always missed the net.

Caroline looked at the ground. "I don't like to wear my glasses. The kids on my other hockey team used to tease me a lot."

Brady shook his head. "Well that's not going to happen on this team. We're the Icehogs, and friends don't tease friends."

Chester nodded in agreement as he pushed his glasses back up his nose.

"You're such a super-fast skater, I bet if you wear your glasses, you'll put that puck in the net today!" Brady told her.

Caroline felt much better. She reached into her hockey bag and put on her glasses.

When everyone had their uniforms on and skates laced up,
they huddled in the center of the room and began their team cheer.

"We've got the power,
We've got the might,
Caroline wears glasses,
And skates like dynamite!"

It was almost the end of the game, and the Icehogs were winning by one goal. Lining up at the face-off circle, Brady could see that Caroline was flustered. She had really hoped to score a big goal to impress her new teammates.

"I guess these glasses aren't helping me at all," she said.

And then it happened.

A Hound player got the puck and headed straight for Chester.
Caroline, the super skater, took off after him.

The Hound player flipped the puck right between Chester's skates, and the Icehogs watched in horror as it went sliding **slooowly** toward the goal line.

In the instant before the puck crossed the line, Caroline lunged forward and whacked it away with her stick.

The buzzer sounded.

Caroline had saved the game for the Icehogs!

In the dressing room, Caroline whispered to Brady.
"Thank you Brady, for making me see that I needed to *see*!"

BRADY BRADY

and the B Team

It was the start of a new hockey season and Brady was excited.
He just knew this would be the best season ever for the Icehogs.

As always, Brady arrived first at the rink, followed by Tes.

The dressing room buzzed with chatter. Everyone was eager to get out on the ice. They would have to work hard, since their first game was tomorrow.

At the start of practice, Coach reviewed the drills on a chalkboard.

"Okay," he called out. "I want you all to loop around the pylons as fast as you can. Then *zip* over here and *zip* over there. Then pass the puck to another player who will take a shot on Chester. Wait a minute! Where is Chester?"

The dressing room fell silent. How were they going to do their drills without a goalie?

"I guess we'll have to cancel our practice," Coach said, shaking his head.

"Wait! One of us could go in net," Brady suggested.

"Yeah!" Tes agreed. "I'll get the spare equipment."

Everyone breathed a sigh of relief. Practice wouldn't be cancelled, after all.

Tree was first to volunteer. He played goalie in street hockey. This couldn't be very different — he thought. Tree thought wrong. The ice was **waaay** too slippery, and the equipment was **waaay** too small.

Caroline tried next, but her glasses kept fogging up. She couldn't see a thing.

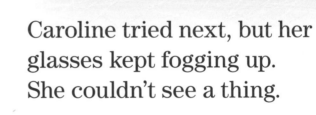

Then Tes took a turn. She twirled and spun, but didn't block a single shot.

Kev went in, but he never stopped talking until Coach asked him to collect all the pucks inside the net.

The first practice of the year was a *disaster*. Everyone was disappointed.

Brady and Tes were saying good-bye outside the rink
when they spotted Chester, running across the parking lot.
"Sorry I'm late!" Chester yelled. He was out of breath and
dropping equipment with every step.

"Late? Practice is over!" said Brady. "Where were you?"

Chester bent to pick up his goalie pads.
"Uh, I just . . . there was something I had to do."

"But it was an important practice," Brady replied.
"Our first game is tomorrow!"

"I'm sorry, Brady Brady. I wanted to be here, but I . . . I slept in."

Chester was making up excuses, but Brady wasn't sure why.

The next morning the dressing room was quiet. Everyone was nervous about the first game of the year — especially after such a horrible practice.

Tree hummed as he adjusted his shoulder pads, Caroline brushed her hair over and over, Kev talked non-stop, and Chester was . . .

. . . MISSING!

"Who'd like to take a turn between the pipes?"
asked Coach, swinging the goalie stick in the air.

Nobody volunteered.

Their knees shook and their teeth chattered as the Icehogs stepped onto the ice. They were playing an annoying team called the Hounds — without a *real* goalie!

It didn't take the Hounds long to start teasing.

"Hey Icehogs! Aren't you gonna say your team cheer?
Here's one for you!"

"We've got the power,
We've got the might,
We're going to lose big
With no goalie in sight!"

The Icehogs did lose big that day . . . **really** big.
It was a terrible way to start the season.

"We got creamed out there," Caroline groaned, "all because of Chester."

"How could he do that to us?" asked Kev. "He really let us down."

Brady didn't like losing, but he refused to believe his friend would hurt the team on purpose. "He must have had a good reason to miss the game," he said.

At school the next day, Kev saw Chester talking to his teacher during recess. He was about to say hello, when he heard Chester say something about joining the **"B team"** and trying to win a championship.

Kev was upset. *Chester? On another hockey team?* he wondered.
That must be why he wasn't at the game yesterday!

On his way home from school, Kev caught up with Brady and told him what he'd overheard. Brady was shocked to learn that Chester was playing for a different hockey team. What would the Icehogs do without him? This would definitely NOT be their best year yet.

Brady could hardly sleep that night. He decided to talk to Chester, first thing in the morning.

Brady was eating breakfast when Hatrick brought in
the morning paper.

Chester's picture was on the front page! Chester was on another team. But it wasn't a hockey team, it was a **_BEE_** team — a **_SPELLING BEE_** team!

Brady ran to the phone. "You're in a Spelling Bee? Why didn't you tell us?"

144

"I didn't think I'd have to. I figured I'd be eliminated before I had to miss any games."

Then Chester whispered, "Besides . . . I was afraid everyone would laugh."

"I think it's great!" said Brady. "We thought you had joined another **hockey** team."

"I'd never be disloyal to the Icehogs," Chester replied. "But what am I going to do? The final round of the Spelling Bee is tonight. I'm so nervous. I hope I can still make it to the game."

"Don't worry about that, Chester," Brady told him. "We'll manage somehow. Good luck with the Spelling Bee."

Brady could hardly wait.
He had one more call to make.

That afternoon, Coach phoned all the Icehogs and asked them to come extra early before the game.

They met outside the arena.

"I'm afraid we may have to play without Chester again tonight," he told them.

Everyone gasped. So it was true! Chester had abandoned the Icehogs!

Coach held up his hand. "Wait," he said. "Brady Brady, why don't you tell them what's going on?"

"Chester's still an Icehog. He's competing in the Spelling Bee finals and he needs our support."

147

The Icehogs ran to the school. The gym was packed with people. Some kids sat in chairs on the stage, but one chair was empty — *Chester's!*

He was hiding backstage. "W-w-what are you guys d-d-doing here?" Chester mumbled through chattering teeth.

"We came to cheer you on, Chester," Brady replied.

"But . . . I . . . what about the game?" asked Chester.

"We can beat the Dragoons anytime," Tes replied. "You're part of our team, and a team sticks together."

Before Chester went on stage they huddled together for their team cheer:
"We've got the power,
We've got the might,
Chester's a great goalie,
Who can spell words right!"

Chester was doing very well when the Icehogs had to leave for their game. Brady gave his friend a thumbs-up as they hurried away.

The dressing room was quiet as the team laced up their skates. The Icehogs wanted Chester to win, but they had secretly hoped he would make the game. Now they would have to play without him — again.

Just then, Coach walked in.
"Listen up," he announced.
"You should all know that Chester is . . .

HERE!"

The Icehogs cheered as Chester dashed through the door. He was holding a gigantic medal and a framed certificate!

"Wow! You won!" Brady yelled.

"Yup! But I couldn't have done it without my team," Chester replied with a big grin.

"I forgot to ask. What was your winning word?"
Chester grinned. *"**Dependability**,"* he said.
"Definition please?" said Brady.
"I-C-E-H-O-G-S!" he spelled. Chester was back, and this really
would be the best season ever.